Heather was born and raised in Stoke-on-Trent, where she worked as a psychiatric nurse until she moved to South West Scotland in 2003. She now lives on a remote smallholding with her five dogs and various other animals and poultry. The idea for this book came from her interest in studying the insects in her garden pond and surrounding wildlife, combined with wanting to help the younger generation learn about the harm that plastic can do and how they can help look after the beautiful planet they live on.

TALES OF MARRDUCK

**Reading/Colouring Book
Educational and Eco-Friendly**

HEATHER BOURNE

ILLUSTRATED BY:
BEVERLEY COOPER

AUSTIN MACAULEY PUBLISHERS™
LONDON • CAMBRIDGE • NEW YORK • SHARJAH

A CIP catalogue record for this title is available from the British Library.

ISBN 9781528951173 (Paperback)
ISBN 9781528951296 (ePub e-book)

www.austinmacauley.com

First Published (2021)
Austin Macauley Publishers Ltd
25 Canada Square
Canary Wharf
London
E14 5LQ

To all wee beasties, stay safe!

I would like to thank my wonderful friend Beverley Cooper for her lovely illustrations. Also to Pam Wright and my family and friends for all the support and encouragement.

Hello! My name is Lady Puddy. I am one of the chosen few, the chief advisor to the clan of Marrduck.

We are one of many clans that can be found at the bottom of a pond where all creatures and people live together.

Marrduck is a place of great mystery where we teach fairness and honesty. As well as healing powers, we also have great magical ability.

I would like to tell you about the time when the lives of all who lived in Marrduck changed forever and the Marrduck Clan began a quest to help our planet.

Welcome to Marrduck, let your journey begin...

"Let's go!" shouted Finnley. "Faster, faster, Taddy!" The TADPOLE taxi whooshed in and out of the pondweed.

"Do a 360-degree turn please, then a double flip with pike. Go, go, go, Taddy, ride that ripple, let's go!" said Megan.

In and out of the BROAD-LEAVED PONDWEED they went, up and down, round and round, faster and faster and faster.

Taddy shouted, "Shall we try the Taddy Tetter's Uppydowny? I dare you!"
"No, no, we always fall off and it messes up my hair," replied Megan.
Bailey said, "Do it, just do it! I have my new lucky blue boots on."
"Oh, I do hope it's a soft landing," replied Alfie.

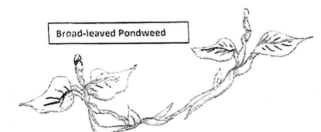

BANG! SPLASH!
Finnley pulled large amounts of broad-leaved pondweed from his dungarees.

Megan said, "Yuk, it's slimy, just look what a mess my hair is and so much for your 'lucky new blue boots'," she said, pointing to Bailey.
Bailey gave a very cheeky grin, saying, "One day we'll do it, won't we, Finnley?" He then winked at his big brother.

Finnley replied, "I do hope so, I'm so fed up with all this crash landing and getting all this slime on my clothes."

As Finnley was trying to get all the slimy weed out of his dungarees, he saw out of the corner of his eye the most cheeky, naughty prank—pulling pond life ever.
"Oh NO! NO! It's THEM!"

"Who do you mean?" said Alfie as he tried to remove slime from his pockets and from under his T—shirt.

"It's the DFs, the Dreadful Funnies, the dragonfly larvae!" said Finnley.

At this point Taddy hit a ripple and sped off.

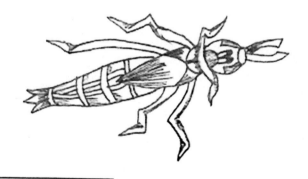

Dragonfly Larva

Finnley shouted, "Come on, let's jump up to the broad—leaved pondweed and swing on it, we can lose them if we keep swinging."
Bailey, Alfie and Megan all followed Finnley, swinging in and out

backwards and forwards on the broad—leaved pondweed. Baily complained about getting more slime on his lucky blue boots and Megan complained about her hair getting messy again.
Finnley told them, "You two will have to stop complaining, it could be worse. My watch is full of slime and it's gone funny. OK, I think we've lost them, we can drop down here."
Baily landed with a *BANG* and Alfie told him to be quiet.
"We don't want the DFs to know where we are."
"It's my lucky new blue boots, they are so heavy!" said Bailey as they heard *SPLASH, SPLASH, SPLASH!*

Alfie noticed that the DFs had surrounded them with a perfect circle. "I never saw them or heard them!" Alfie whispered as water was hitting them from every angle.

"Ouch, ooh, argh, ow, my hair, my lucky new blue boots, fish nuts, my watch has gone funny now. TADDY, TADDY, TADDY, HELP US!"

They were all shouting at once. "Help us, we have been pranked!"

WHOOSH! Taddy appeared out of nowhere. "Don't worry, I'll get you all." He went around and picked them up one by one.

"Please get us out of here quickly," said Finnley.

"Wow, you caught that ripple well!" said Alfie.

"I'm not known as the Rapid Rippling Taddy for nothing, nobody can ride the ripples like me!"

As they swam around Marrduck, Bailey noticed that his watch was going backwards. He told the others and they all looked at their watches. All the watches were going backwards, but still told the right time.

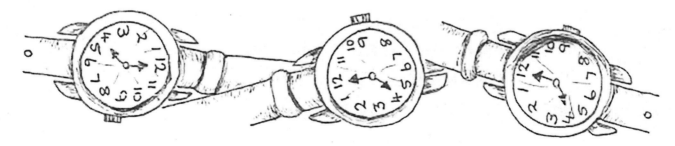

"That's very strange," said Taddy. "I think Marrduck is trying to tell you all something. It's very odd that a watch goes backwards but tells the right time."

He then shouted, "Look, look, up there! The WHIRLING BEETLES are spinning faster and faster at the top of the pond! There must be something wrong I wonder what it is. They are our 'looker overs', they let us know when anything is wrong.

"Their eyes are split in two so the top half can see above the water and the bottom half can see under the water surface. Hang on, kids, I'm going to shoot up the top and see what's happening."

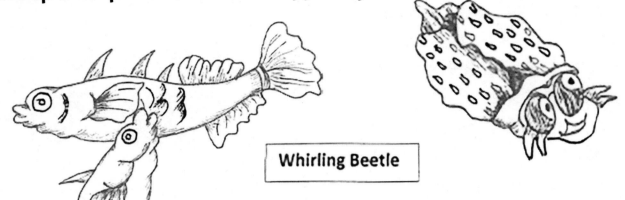

Whirling Beetle

WHOOSH! Up and up they went and when they reached the top, Alfie asked the whirling beetles what was wrong.

Wattie, the leader of the whirling beetles, told them that Mary and Malcolm, the STICKLEBACKS, had come upstream for a swim and the worst of the worst that had ever taken place in Marrduck had now happened. When everyone looked down, they realised that Mary and Malcolm had been caught up in a PLASTIC CARRIER BAG.

Sticklebacks

They were stuck in the corner of the bag at the bottom of the pond and some rocks had fallen and trapped them.

"It's those Above People chucking their rubbish everywhere and it's usually horrible plastic," said Finnley. "Will they ever learn to look after this beautiful planet? They are choking and poisoning everything, they are all so 'shellfish'. Right, we'll work together and get this sorted out. We'll have to get Mary and Malcolm out quickly if we are to save them. Whirling beetles, please take us to Mary and Malcolm to see what we can do."

"Of course we will, that's our job," said the whirling beetles.

When they arrived at the scene, they saw the most horrible and terrible sight. A large plastic carrier bag was held down with rocks.
"We swam in by mistake," shouted a very distressed Mary, "then the rocks fell and trapped us. Please, please help us get out."
After a quick conversation, the kids decided to call for Greta the GREAT DIVING BEETLE because she had a really powerful mouth.

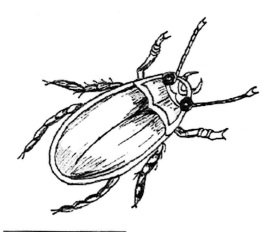

Great Diving Beetle

Megan jumped onto Taddy's back and off they went to Greta's home at the top of the pond.

"You're hitting the ripples at some speed again, Taddy," said Megan. "Love it!"

As they reached the top of the pond, Megan spotted Greta and told her what had happened.

"Right," said Greta, "let's get this sorted out." She took a great big gasp of air, swoosh, she swam down to the pond floor following Megan and Taddy.

"What a horrible thing plastic is!" exclaimed Greta.

"Don't worry, we can get you out!" Greta told Mary and Malcolm.

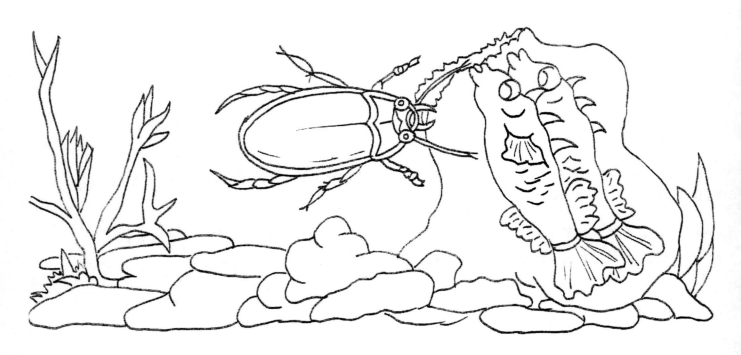

She was soon chewing on the plastic bag with her powerful mouth. *Chew, chew, chew, rip, rip, rip.*

Yes, it had worked, Greta had freed Mary and Malcolm!

"Thank you, thank you, thanks to all of you. This plastic is evil. We were so frightened, what sort of people use this horrible stuff?"

"Thank you all so much, we hope we never see any plastic stuff ever again," said Mary.

Alfie said, "Right, let's get rid of this plastic bag, it does not belong in Marrduck."

"Sir, sir" the WATERBOATMAN, the postman, said. "Right, I can take the plastic bag to the top of the pond at the edge of Marrduck if that would help?"

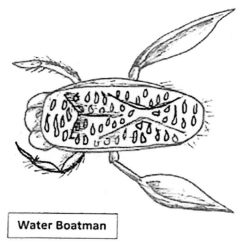

Water Boatman

Alfie said, "Yes please, and it's time for us to do the Marrduck Magic."

"Oh yes. Let's get this evil plastic bag gone for good," said Bailey.

The four of them jumped onto Taddy, who said, "Hold on, let's ride those ripples."

WHOOSH! Up and up they went and all their friends shouted good luck as they raced up to the top. As they neared the top, Megan shouted, "Are you ready, lads?"

"Yes, yes, yes, let's do this!" the lads shouted back. As they splashed through the water, they all shouted together the magic words: "Marrduck, Marrduck!"

"Wow, we are on top of the pond," said Bailey.

Taddy turned around, leaving them at the pond edge, and zoomed back down to Marrduck

"Right, let's see if we can get our friends Muckyduck and Dirtyduck to come and help us," said Finnley.

"Marrduck, Marrduck!" they all shout again together.

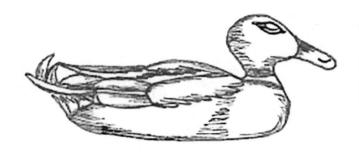

Nothing happened.
"Marrduck, Marrduck!" they all shouted again.
SPLISH! SPLASH! "Hello, you lot, how's it flowing down there?" asked Muckyduck.

"Bad at the moment," said Alfie, explaining what had just happened to Mary and Malcolm.

"Oh, here's an odd thing too," said Bailey, "our watches are going backwards but telling the right time."
"Well, it's perhaps not as strange as you think. Time will tell," said Muckyduck. "So would you like us to help you get rid of the plastic bag?"
"Yes, please!" said the kids.

"Right, jump on our backs and show us where the plastic bag is."
SPLISH! SPLASH! Muckyduck and Dirtyduck start swimming across the pond.

Megan complained, "Oh no! Here we go again, my hair's a mess!"

"Well, that's nothing, you should see the mess of my new blue boots," Bailey said to her.

"I can see the bag," said Dirtyduck, "let's get it!"

"Got it!" shouted Muckyduck. "OK, let's go. Hold tight, kids, this could be a bit rough, we're not that good at taking off and not much better at landing either."

"Here we go! Muckyduck, let's give it some welly!" cried Dirtyduck. *WHOOSH, WHOOSH! FLAP, FLAP!* They were finally up.

"It's windy up here," said Finnley.

"Shush, it isn't that bad, at least it's blowing the sludge off my new blue boots, but my watch is still going backwards," Bailey said. Up, up and up they flew.

"Wow its great up here," said Megan. "Yes, it's not bad," said Muckyduck. "We don't do a lot of flying, we tend to swim mostly, but it is good, you can see lots from up here."

"Shoe shop!" shouted Bailey. "Look at those boots, I love them. Wow, look at all those shops!"

Dirtyduck told them they were going along Newton Norton High Street, which was an interesting village.

"Look, bins! I see bins!" shouted Alfie. "Can we take the plastic bag and drop it into a bin? There's one outside the post office we can use."
"Hold tight," Dirtyduck instructed them as he whooshed quickly down to the bin. He took aim and, BANG, into the bin went the plastic bag.
"Good shot!" Alfie said as Dirtyduck got the plastic bag into the bin the first time.

"It's easy," said Muckyduck, "we ducks happen to have a very good aim."
"We will remember that," said Alfie,

"job well done, thank you!" shouted all the kids.
"Right, it's time to get you kids home," quacked the ducks.
In the blink of an eye, they were all back at the top of Marrduck Pond.
Well, it's safe to say that it was a bit of a rough landing. Megan's hair was all over the place and Bailey's new blue boots were covered in mud.

"Thank you, Dirtyduck and Muckyduck, for helping us rescue Mary and Malcolm and get rid of that evil plastic bag."
"It's not a problem, kids, we're always here to help."

The kids shouted, "Marrduck, Marrduck" as Muckyduck and Dirtyduck swam away across the pond

Taddy appeared.

MARRDUCK   MARRDUCK

"Right, let's get you kids home. Jump on and hold tight."
Off through the ripples they went. when they arrived home, all their mums and dads were waiting with villagers. Everyone was applauding loudly.
Baily said, "Oh no, everybody is looking at us and I've still got mud all over my new blue boots."

"Well, look at my hair, it's so messy," said Megan.
"Shhh, stop complaining, look who's here," whispered Finnley.
"Oh, help me get the mud off my new blue boots," said Bailey, "here's Lady Puddy."

Lady Puddy was a chocolate Labrador.
"Wow!" Finnley whispered. "Our great leader, the one who teaches us to show compassion for others."
Marrduck was a magical and mystical place where Lady Puddy taught fairness, honesty, healing and magic. She raised her left paw and everyone went quiet.
"I would like to thank these four young people of Marrduck who helped us rid our pond of the evil plastic bag, you showed great courage and compassion and I thank you all!"

Just as Lady Puddy began to speak again, Finnley said, "Lady Puddy, please may I ask you a question?"

"Of course, you may."

"Could you explain why all of our watches are going backwards but telling the right time?"

"Well," Lady Puddy told him, "the people of Marrduck wished that you Finnley, Alfie, Bailey and Megan could be granted the most special powers that anyone could imagine so that in the future you can work with us, the people of Marrduck, in trying to turn back time to when our beautiful planet was not being poisoned by this evil plastic. Your watches are a constant reminder of cleaner times gone by. Remember our motto of Marrduck: LOVE LIFE, RESPECT LIFE (AMARE VITA QUANTUM VITA)."

Here's a clue to the next adventure in Marrduck

Coming soon in *More Tales from Marrduck*

Can you find the secret message?

P=PAGE	L=LINE	W=WORD
P–18	L–17	W–6
P–20	L–9	W–3
P–7	L–11	W–14
P–18	L–15	W–8
P–11	L–6	W–1
P–9	L–18	W–8
P–20	L–09	W–3
P–17	L–01	W–13

????????????

P–20	L–11	W–5
P–9	L–23	W–2
P–21	L–6	W–7
P–16	L–3	W–1

????????????